DRIVE THRU

THE CALL FOR
COFFEE

by Harriet Brundle

The Coffee Stop

BEARPORT
PUBLISHING

Minneapolis, Minnesota

Credits

All images are courtesy of Shutterstock.com, unless otherwise specified.
With thanks to Getty Images, Thinkstock Photo, and iStockphoto.

Cover images – Evikka, Rabilbanimilbu, Nikita Emelianov, Evikka. Recurring images – vikka, Rabilbanimilbu, Nikita Emelianov, Evikka, Macrovector, MIKHAIL GRACHIKOV, Steve Morfi. Page 6 – Mitidieri Comunicacoes. 7 – Szymon Apanowicz. 8 – RachenArt. 9 – Somchai_Stock. 10 – alfotokunst. 11 – Athirati. 12 – bonga1965. 13 – whitehoune. 14 – Dreamer Company. 15 – Vital Safo. 16 – Diana Taliun. 17 – mavo. 18 – Olena Yakobchuk. 19 – NakoPhotography. 20 – Redrock Photography. 21 – StudioByTheSea, razzel, multiart, bogdanhoda. 23 – Mountain Brothers.

Library of Congress Cataloging-in-Publication Data

Names: Brundle, Harriet, author.
Title: The call for coffee / by Harriet Brundle.
Description: Fusion books. | Minneapolis, MN : Bearport Publishing Company, [2022] | Series: Drive thru | Includes bibliographical references and index.
Identifiers: LCCN 2021011420 (print) | LCCN 2021011421 (ebook) | ISBN 9781647479466 (library binding) | ISBN 9781647479541 (paperback) | ISBN 9781647479626 (ebook)
Subjects: LCSH: Coffee--Processing--Juvenile literature.
Classification: LCC TP645 .B78 2022 (print) | LCC TP645 (ebook) | DDC 663/.93--dc23
LC record available at https://lccn.loc.gov/2021011420
LC ebook record available at https://lccn.loc.gov/2021011421

For more information, write to Bearport Publishing, 5357 Penn Avenue South, Minneapolis, MN 55419. Printed in the United States of America.

CONTENTS

THE CALL FOR COFFEE

Coffee is made from coffee beans. The beans are grown in many places, including Colombia, Vietnam, and Brazil.

The Coffee Stop

Coffee beans grow in fields.

The three kinds of coffee beans are Arabica, Robusta, and Liberica.

Different kinds of coffee beans are grown in different countries. Each kind of bean has its own taste.

IN THE FIELD

Coffee plant

Coffee beans are actually seeds. The seeds are planted and grow into coffee plants.

The Coffee Stop

The plants grow fruit called coffee cherries. The cherries are bright red. People **harvest** the cherries.

In some places, people pick coffee cherries by hand. In others, people use machines.

GETTING THE BEANS

Each cherry has a coffee bean inside. People work to get the beans out. Sometimes they use water to wash away the fruit part of the cherries, so only the beans are left.

The Coffee Stop

Another way is to leave the cherries outside so the hot sun dries them out.

DRYING CHERRIES

AT THE FACTORY

After the cherries dry, they go into a machine. This machine takes away the fruit part and leaves the beans.

The beans can be sorted by hand or by a machine.

Next, the beans are sorted at a factory. Beans that are not good enough to make coffee are taken away.

13

TASTE TEST

To become coffee, the beans must be **roasted**. A small number of beans may be tested first.

A cup of coffee is made for the test. A taster drinks it. If it tastes good, then the rest of the beans will be roasted.

15

READY TO ROAST

Roasted beans

Unroasted beans

Roasting the beans turns them from green to dark brown.

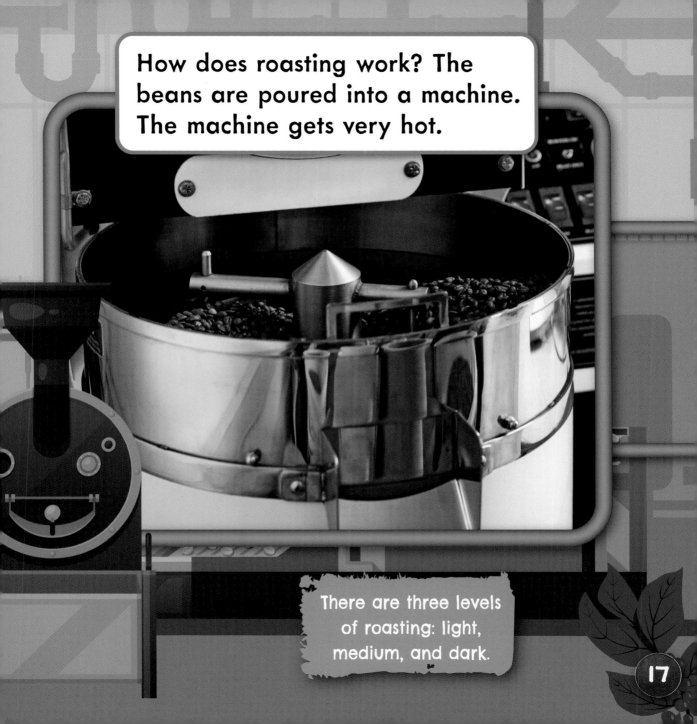

How does roasting work? The beans are poured into a machine. The machine gets very hot.

There are three levels of roasting: light, medium, and dark.

17

GETTING THE RIGHT TASTE

The taste of coffee depends on how long the beans are roasted. It also depends on how hot they get.

Beans cooling

After the beans have been roasted, they are cooled.

THE FINAL STEP

The roasted beans are then put into a machine. The machine **grinds** them into **powder.**

GROUND COFFEE

FRENCH PRESS

COFFEE MAKER

PERCOLATOR
(PUR-KUH-LAY-TUR)

The ground coffee must be **brewed** to drink. Hot water is passed over the ground coffee. This can be done with a coffee maker, French press, or percolator. Then, the coffee is ready!

COFFEE TIME!

I hope you enjoyed our trip! We've come back with enough coffee to make lots of tasty drinks. *Yum!*

The Coffee St[o]

* **MENU** *

Americano

Espresso

Latte

Mocha

23

GLOSSARY

brewed made into a drink by passing through hot water

grinds breaks into very tiny pieces

harvest to pick or gather plants that are to be used by humans

powder many tiny pieces of something

roasted cooked in a way that gets very hot and dry

INDEX